For Tilly

The BOY GIANT
©2009
by
Allan
Plenderleith

First published in hardback by
Ravette Publishing Limited 2009.

Reprinted in paperback 2010.

ISBN: 978-1-84161-352-9

The Boy Giant

by Allan Plenderleith

Mr and Mrs Small loved each other very much.

lumpy the dog

mrs. small

mr. small

The one thing they wanted more than anything in the world was to have a baby.

Then one magical day it happened.

The doctor told Mrs Small she had
a tiny baby in her tummy.

The baby in her tummy grew
bigger and bigger
and
BIGGER.

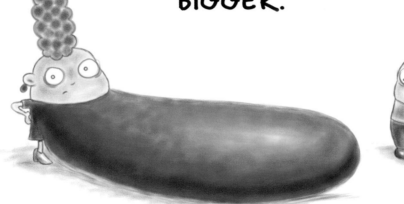

Until one day it was ready to
meet the world...

It was a boy.
A very BIG boy.

They decided to call him
HUJO.

He was so big he couldn't even
fit in his cot.

And he was too big for ordinary
nappies. They had to use
bath towels!

And what was inside the nappies?

Giant, enormous, huge...
Well, the less said about that
the better.

But Hujo had a big appetite too.
He drank so much milk they
had to buy a whole herd of cows.

And Hujo grew bigger and bigger
and
BIGGER.

Soon Hujo was too big to
fit in the house.

So Mr Small turned the garage
into a lovely new room.

Hujo was a bit lonely,
so Mrs Small made him a
friend to keep him company.

Hujo loved playing in the park.

But he was so big
he broke the swing.

And the slide.

And the roundabout.

Hujo wasn't allowed in
the park anymore.

And Hujo grew bigger
and bigger
and BIGGER!

Soon it was time to start big boy school.

my little
boy,
all grown up

Hujo couldn't fit through
the school doors, so he had to listen
from outside

...whatever the weather.

Hujo loved playing football.

But when he kicked the ball...

He was good in goal though.

But Hujo wasn't very happy.

He was too big to play with the
other boys and girls.

And worse, he was even too big
to get a proper hug.

Hujo was all alone.

Soon word of Hujo's enormous
size travelled across the world.

Then one day, just after breakfast,
the phone rang.

"Good morning. I'm the President of
America," said the voice.

"Hujo! We need your help! There's a giant monster attacking the city!" said the President.

Please! Come quickly!

Hujo knew he was the only one
who could help.

So he set off on his big adventure.

With the help of some little
boats, Hujo set off across the sea.

It took a long time.

But Hujo got bigger and bigger
and BIGGER.

So big that the little boats sank!
And Hujo couldn't swim.

Suddenly, Hujo felt something
beneath him.

He was very frightened.

It was a whale!
She lifted Hujo onto her back and
took him all the way to America!

Finally he arrived,
passing a toy lady holding an ice cream
on the way.

The President arrived in his
helicopter. "Hujo! It's hiding somewhere
in the city," he said. "A giant monster!"

Hujo tiptoed carefully through the city, being careful not to stand on any of the little yellow cars.

All was quiet. Until suddenly, Hujo
jumped at a strange sound.

Hujo followed the sound to a nice little garden. Something was curled up into a ball.

It was big and green and covered in purple spots. It was...

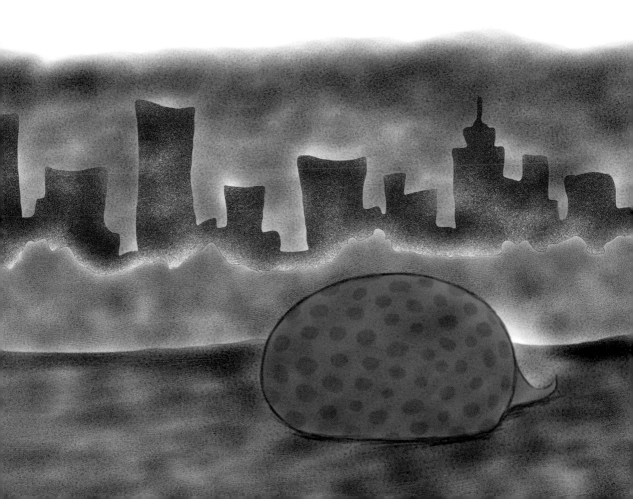

A little girl! A BIG little girl!

"Hello!" said Hujo. "You're not a monster!"
The little girl turned, wiped the tears
from her eyes and smiled.

"You're just like me," giggled the girl.
Hujo giggled too.

Suddenly they realised they weren't
alone any more.

And for the first time in both their lives, they each got a great big hug.

Hujo told the President there was no monster, just a frightened BIG little girl.

From that day on, Hujo and Bigsy
became the best of friends.

Sometimes Bigsy came to visit Hujo at his place.

Sometimes Hujo went to visit Bigsy at her place.

But wherever they were,
their love just got bigger and bigger
and BIGGER.